MONSTER HOUSE™

DJ'S NOTEBOOK

by Tom Mason and Dan Danko

Simon Spotlight
New York   London   Toronto   Sydney

SIMON SPOTLIGHT
An imprint of Simon & Schuster
Children's Publishing Division
1230 Avenue of the Americas, New York, New York 10020
© 2006 by Columbia Pictures Industries, Inc.
All Rights Reserved.
SIMON SPOTLIGHT and colophon are registered trademarks
of Simon & Schuster, Inc.
First Edition
2 4 6 8 10 9 7 5 3 1
ISBN-13: 978-1-4169-1816-5
ISBN-10: 1-4169-1816-7

OCTOBER 30

All right! One more day before the big day—Halloween! I can't wait for all the free candy and chocolate. I love trick-or-treating, but there's one house I will NEVER go to: my neighbor Mr. Nebbercracker's house. He probably has something awful planned. He's always up to something scary or mean for Halloween.

He's got that perfect lawn he never lets anyone step on. I've been watching him and his house for a long time. There's definitely something very strange going on over there.

Today I took a picture of Mr. Nebbercracker taking a tricycle into his house. He stole it from a little girl! Can you believe it? He takes *everything* that lands on his lawn—and they're all gone forever! Response time today was the same as yesterday: fourteen seconds. I wrote it down in my logbook.

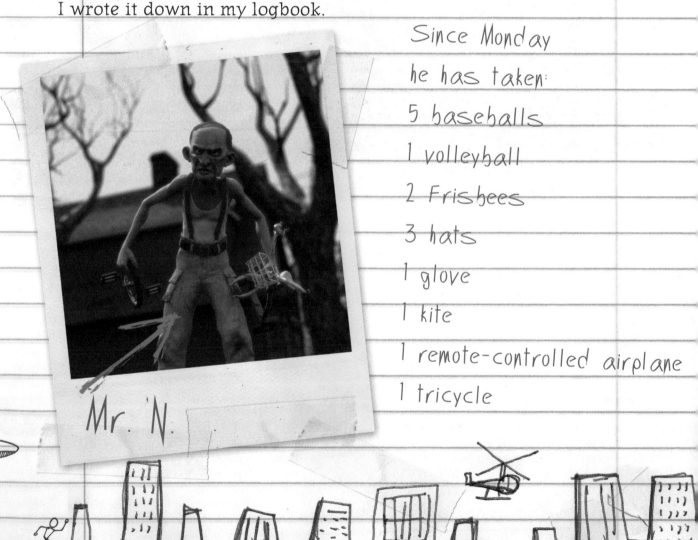

Mr. N.

Since Monday he has taken:

5 baseballs

1 volleyball

2 Frisbees

3 hats

1 glove

1 kite

1 remote-controlled airplane

1 tricycle

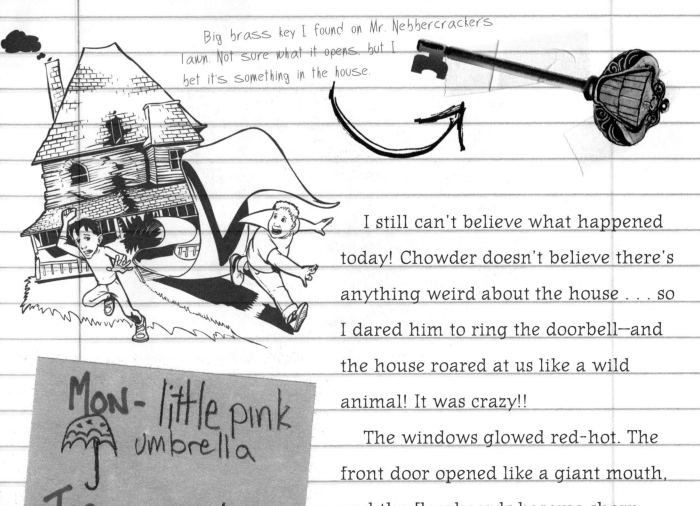

Big brass key I found on Mr. Nebbercracker's lawn. Not sure what it opens, but I bet it's something in the house.

MON - little pink umbrella

Tues - a cool metal robot

WN took Sue Bloom's Pogo Stick — I got a picture!

I still can't believe what happened today! Chowder doesn't believe there's anything weird about the house . . . so I dared him to ring the doorbell—and the house roared at us like a wild animal! It was crazy!!

The windows glowed red-hot. The front door opened like a giant mouth, and the floorboards became sharp wooden teeth!! The carpet shot out like a tongue and tried to get us! We were so scared. I knew there was something bad about that house!

Chowder   me

nebbercraker

I think I killed him . . . Mr. Nebbercracker, that is. He ran after us like a madman, yelling and shaking his fist. I thought his head was gonna pop. Instead he just fell to the ground, right on top of me! The ambulance came and took him away. Hope he's okay . . .

FRACTIONS

HOMEWORK
P. 89-93

OCTOBER 31

Halloween morning. Chowder and I have been watching the Monster House all night through the telescope, but the house didn't move. What are we going to do? Trick-or-treating is just eight hours away.

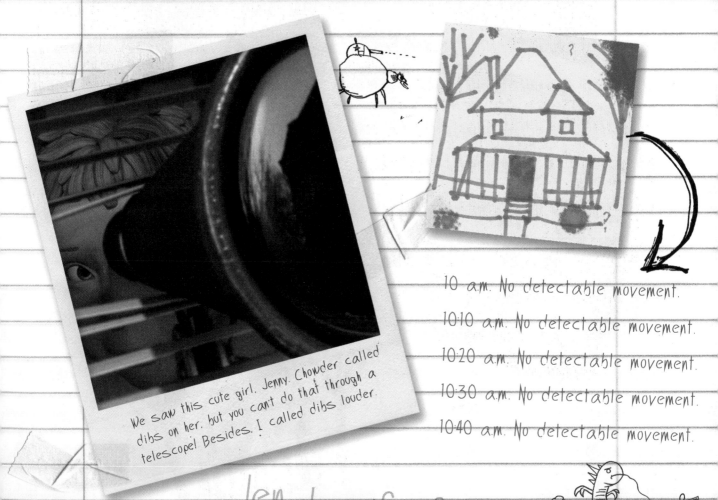

We saw this cute girl, Jenny. Chowder called dibs on her, but you can't do that through a telescope! Besides, I called dibs louder.

10 a.m. No detectable movement.
10:10 a.m. No detectable movement.
10:20 a.m. No detectable movement.
10:30 a.m. No detectable movement.
10:40 a.m. No detectable movement.

Jenny Jen Jennifer?

Jenny was heading right for Mr. Nebbercracker's house! She didn't know the horrible things the house could do, but *we* did! We had to stop her, or the house was going to eat her!

Too late! 10:45 a.m. Detectable movement!

The sidewalk buckled up and pushed Jenny into her wagon. She rolled toward the front door that opened like it was going to eat her. Chowder and I raced onto the lawn and pulled Jenny out of the wagon—just in time!

We knew we couldn't stop the house by ourselves. So we went to the Smartest Guy We Know—Skull, the pizza-delivery dude at Pizza Freek *and* three-time tristate, over-fourteen *Thou Art Dead* champion.

Local Youth Excells at Video Arcade Gaming

Onlookers stunned

Skull told us the secret: To stop the Monster House we had to find its heart. We figured that was the furnace, which was probably in the basement. How come the scariest stuff is always in the basement?

He can help us defeat the house!

He knows *everything* about ghosts and monsters and haunted houses. He explained that sometimes a human spirit can become part of a house and turn it into a monster. Now *that's* creepy.

We went back to my house to come up with a plan.

And the plan was this:

1. Build a dummy to look like a trick-or-treater.
2. Fill the dummy with a few gallons of cold medicine.
3. Feed the dummy to the House.
4. House eats medicine.
5. House goes to sleep.
6. We go in, put out the fire, and get out.

So we created a dummy out of an old vacuum cleaner. It looked just like a real trick-or-treater! It did! Well, kinda.

It worked! Almost.

We sent the dummy moving toward the house, and it was about to make it, but just when the house was about to eat it, the police showed up! Their car ran over the extension cord and pulled the plug! So close!

We told Officers Landers and Lister about the house, but they didn't believe us. No one ever believes kids about monsters. They went to check on the house to prove we were wrong—and that's when the Monster House ate them!

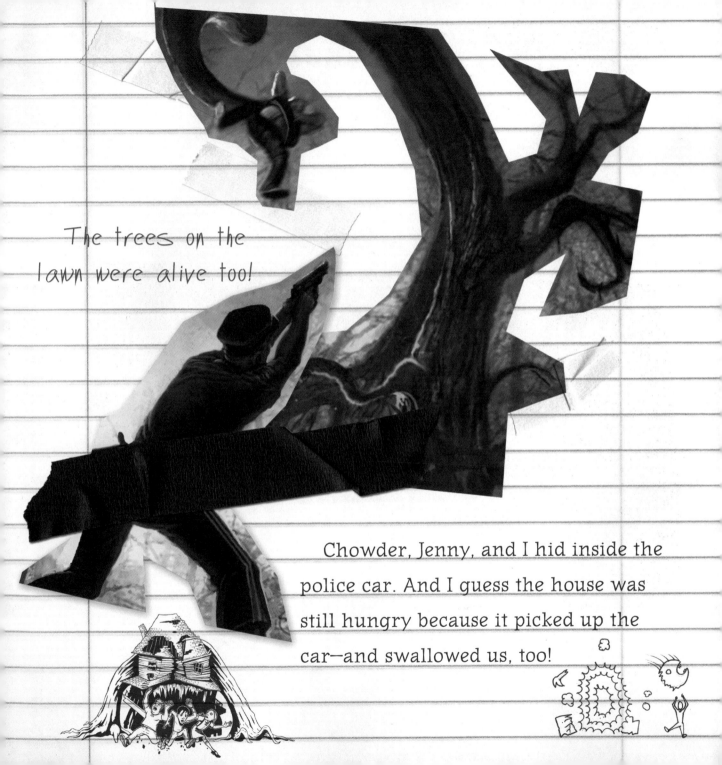

The trees on the lawn were alive too!

Chowder, Jenny, and I hid inside the police car. And I guess the house was still hungry because it picked up the car—and swallowed us, too!

We crashed into the basement, and we couldn't believe what we saw. There was a gigantic pile of all the stuff that Mr. Nebbercracker had taken over the years—baseballs, boomerangs, Slinkys, toy cars, tennis shoes, kites . . . everything was here!

But there was also something behind the toys. It was a circus caravan car for CONSTANCE: THE GIANTESS! The door was padlocked, but I remembered I still had the big brass key. It fit perfectly! I unlocked the caravan door and went inside.

There were posters all over. Mr. Nebbercracker's wife had been a circus performer. Then there was some kind of accident, and she was buried under the house. *This* house! We knew the secret: Constance was Mr. Nebbercracker's wife, and she had become the house!

The house found us! She knew we were inside! The floors rattled and the walls cracked. Wood splintered all over. Pipes burst through the walls. We were terrified!

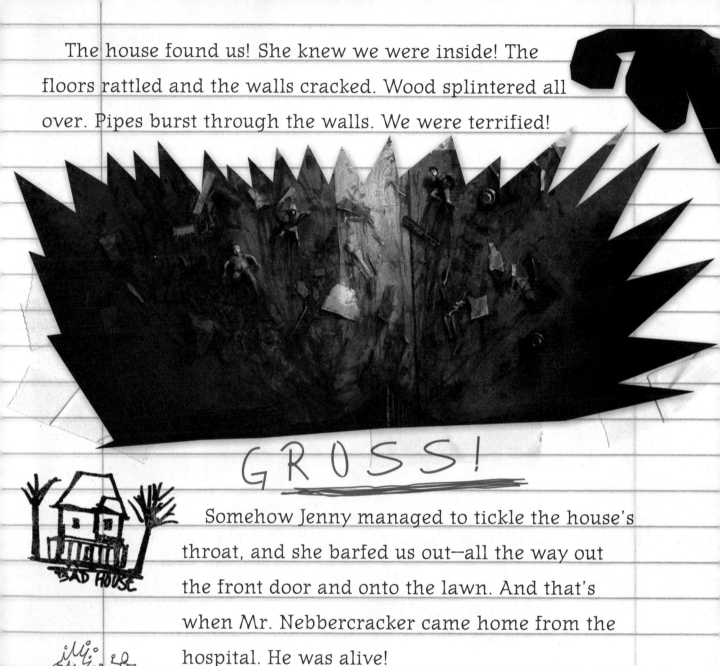

GROSS!

Somehow Jenny managed to tickle the house's throat, and she barfed us out—all the way out the front door and onto the lawn. And that's when Mr. Nebbercracker came home from the hospital. He was alive!

And we were in trouble.

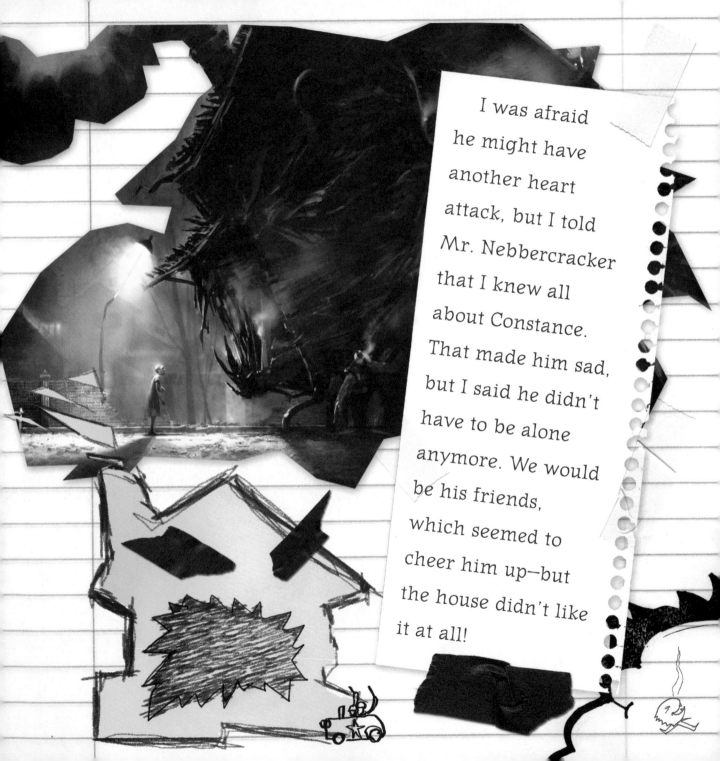

I was afraid he might have another heart attack, but I told Mr. Nebbercracker that I knew all about Constance. That made him sad, but I said he didn't have to be alone anymore. We would be his friends, which seemed to cheer him up—but the house didn't like it at all!

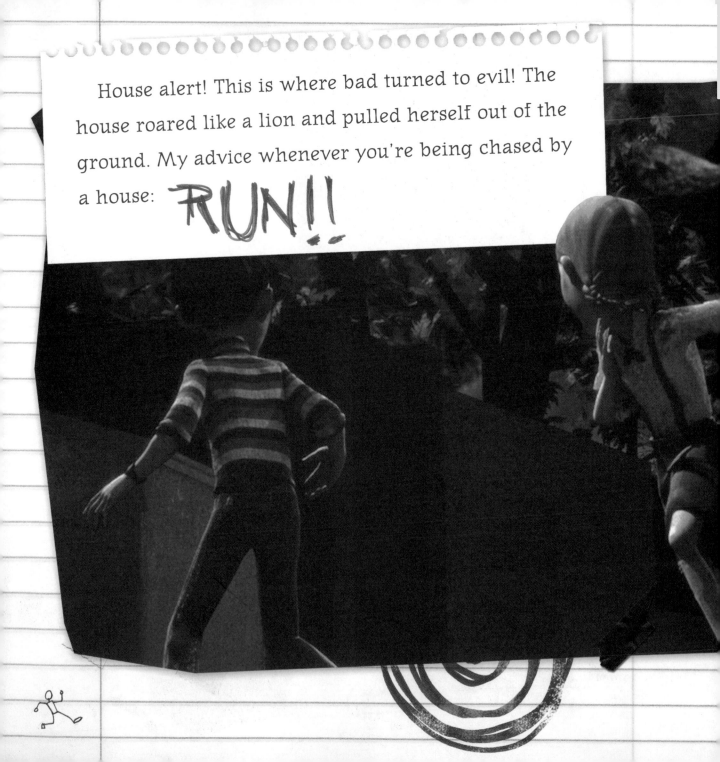

House alert! This is where bad turned to evil! The house roared like a lion and pulled herself out of the ground. My advice whenever you're being chased by a house: **RUN!!**

And we did. Mr. Nebbercracker ran too. We passed some kids getting ready to trick-or-treat, and we knew time was running out. We *had* to stop the house!

Then Mr. N. pulled a bundle of dynamite out of his pocket and lit it. The house was furious!

Chowder, Jenny, and I ran to the construction site and found a backhoe. Chowder got into the cab and shifted the gears. They grinded like he was breaking them, but we were soon on our way to fight the house!

Chowder jerked the backhoe forward and rammed it into the house. Push! Shove! The two beasts went at it like angry wrestlers. And as the house fought back, she pushed Mr. Nebbercracker into some bushes. Mr. Nebbercracker handed me the dynamite—to finish what he had started!

Great. Now *I* had to blow up the house! But I had an idea. There was a really tall crane at the construction site. I was nervous, but I made it to the top of the crane and carefully dropped the dynamite down the house's chimney. Score! The dynamite rolled into the furnace, right into the heart of the Monster House.

Ka-boom! The house exploded! The walls buckled, the windows shattered, and the house fell to the ground. Constance was finally freed from the house—and so was Mr. Nebbercracker. Halloween was saved!

And you know what? This ended up being the best Halloween ever! With Mr. Nebbercracker's help we gave out all the toys the house had collected over the years. No tricks, lots of treats! We were heroes! And I think Jenny likes me better than Chowder . . .

HAPPY HALLOWEEN!